Clifford's
KITTEN

Story and pictures by Norman Bridwell

SCHOLASTIC INC.

New York

For Justin Bryant

ISBN 0-590-58283-6

Copyright © 1984 by Norman Bridwell.
All rights reserved. Published by Scholastic Inc.
CLIFFORD and the CLIFFORD logo are registered trademarks of Norman Bridwell.
SCHOLASTIC HARDCOVER is a registered trademark of Scholastic Inc.

12 11 10 9 8 7 6 5 4 3 2 1   9   5 6 7 8 9/9 0/0

Mom said we could keep him
until we found his owners.

He was so small that Mom said he could sleep in my room.

He slept in the basket Clifford had used

for a bed when he was a puppy.

I think Clifford was a little jealous.

That night Clifford slept as close to me
as he could get.

Mom said the kitten would have to sleep

out next to Clifford until his owners came to get him.

He was a playful little kitten.
He chased butterflies.

Clifford chased butterflies too.

He saw a very big one.

He caught it.

Dad paid the boy for his kite.

Kittens love to play with spools.

Clifford had never played with a spool.

He found one in the street.

Oh my, Clifford was too strong.

We bought fancy cat foods.

The kitten just turned up his nose at them.

Thank goodness,
Clifford isn't a picky eater.

I took the kitten for a ride
in my doll carriage.
I never did that for Clifford.

Clifford wanted a ride too.

While I was explaining why I couldn't push him...

...the kitten jumped out of the carriage
and started across the street.

Clifford was right there.

The kitten didn't even say,
"Thank you."
He just sharpened his claws.

Clifford tried to sharpen his claws.

Oooops.

While Clifford was busy putting the light pole back,
a big dog came into our yard
and growled at the kitten.

He didn't notice Clifford.

The big dog decided to go back to his house to play.

While I was hugging the kitten, a little boy rode up. He said, "Oh, you found my cat. Thank you! I've been looking all over for him."

That sure was a cute kitten.

I hated to see him go.

Oh well, I still have
a pretty good dog.